The Read with Grandma Collection

Collection

Sandy Creek
NEW YORK

CONTENTS

Archie's Bag of Treasures 3

There's No Place Like Home 24

The Littlest Dragon 46

The Greedy Rainbow 68

The Lion Who Lost His Roar 90

The Snake Who Said Shhh.......................... 112

Superchimp 134

Snip Snap Croc 155

Archie's Bag of Treasures

Written and illustrated by
Lucy Barnard

"Look at my gift bag!" Oliver said excitedly. And he pulled out a beautiful silver pinwheel.

"I don't want to see your silly bag," said Archie in a huff.

Archie's big brother Oliver had been to a party, but Archie wasn't invited.

"Oh, Archie, don't be like that," said Mommy. "Let's find a bag and put in some lovely things just for you."

"Yes, please!" agreed Archie.

6

Archie found a perfect **glossy chestnut.**

"This is the first special thing for my bag!"
he told Mommy excitedly, and in it went.

A beautiful
red leaf

sailed down from
the sky and
landed right on
Archie's nose.

"This is the
second thing!"
Archie said.

He found some sweet, juicy blackberries.
One went in his bag and one in his mouth.

Scrumptious!

Archie spotted some **thistles** and asked Mommy to pick him one.

"It reminds me of Sam Hedgehog," he chuckled.

They were heading for home when Archie noticed something hidden in the tufty grass.

It was a beautiful **glass marble** that glittered in the sunshine.

Archie popped it
into his bag.

But just then,
with a *flapping* of wings
and a shrill CAW,
a huge magpie
swooped down.

The magpie had seen the marble glinting in the light.
It snatched Archie's bag and flew off into the sky.

"What can we do, Mommy?"
Archie cried out.

"I don't know, my love…" began Mommy, but she was interrupted by a loud shout.

16

"HEY MAGPIE, LOOK OVER HERE!"

17

The bird whirled around and flew toward Oliver, who was holding his silver pinwheel.

The bird dropped Archie's bag, grabbed the silver pinwheel, and flew away.

"WOW!
You were amazing!"
said Archie.

Safely back in their little house, they all sat down for a tasty snack, and Oliver shared the cake from his gift bag.

"Sorry I was mean to you earlier," said Archie.
"You're the best brother ever!"

And he reached into his bag
and pulled out the marble.
"I'd like you to have this."

"Let's share it," said Oliver, and
they both scampered off to play.

At bedtime, Mommy tucked them in.

"Oliver's bag is almost empty now,"
said Archie with a yawn.

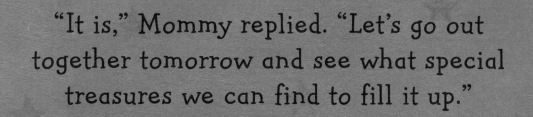

"It is," Mommy replied. "Let's go out together tomorrow and see what special treasures we can find to fill it up."

Archie and Oliver both agreed that was a very good idea indeed.

24

There's No Place Like Home

Dubravka Kolanovic

William loved taking long walks

with his Mom and Dad.

And every evening, when the stars appeared in the sky, his Mom and Dad took turns reading him

a **bedtime story.**

One day, Mom and Dad shared some happy news with William.

Before long, a baby brother arrived. William was **very excited.**

But now Mom
and Dad were
busy all the time.

And when they
forgot his bedtime
stories, William was
sad. He thought
his parents didn't
love him anymore.

William wanted to find a new home.
So he picked up his book and left.

William found his friends, the ducklings, waddling through the forest. "What's wrong?" they asked.

"I'm looking for a new home," he said.

"Come with us to our lake," the ducklings said. "It's very pretty."

The lake was pretty, but William was worried about his book getting wet.

Next, William met his
friend Little Mouse.

"Come with me to my
mouse hole," Little
Mouse suggested.
"It's very cozy."

Little Mouse's mouse hole was cozy, but it was far too small for William and his book to fit inside!

William then met his friend, Little Wolf.

"Come with me to my cave," Little Wolf said. "It's **big** enough for both of us."

Little Wolf's cave was very roomy,
but it was too dark for William to read.

The sun was setting, and William
was still looking for a home.

He felt a friendly wing on his shoulder.

It was Owl! "Come to
my nest," Owl said.
"I LOVE reading!"

William followed
Owl, but when he
arrived at Owl's nest,
it was too high.

William felt lonely. It was dark, and he was scared. The stars appeared in the night sky.

He missed his home and family.
But just then, he heard some familiar voices.

41

It was Mom, Dad, and his little brother!

"William, thank goodness you're safe!"
said Mom and Dad.

"Sorry for leaving," said William.

"Now I know there is no place like home, because home is where my family is!"

43

44

Even though it was
late when they got home,
William and his family did
not go to sleep right away.

After all, Mom and Dad
had to catch up on all the
bedtime stories he had missed.

THE Littlest DRAGON

Susan Quinn

Illustrated by Ag Jatkowska

Long ago, when dragons roamed Earth,
Mrs. Dragon sat waiting for her eggs to hatch.

She smiled as the first egg went CRACK!

She smiled as the second egg went CRACK!

But when the third egg went CRACK...

49

Mrs. Dragon gasped.
Out popped the littlest dragon
she had ever seen.

"Mama!"
said the
Littlest Dragon.

"Aren't you sweet?"
Mrs. Dragon said.

52

"Dragons aren't sweet!"
snorted Mr. Dragon.
"They're big and strong!"

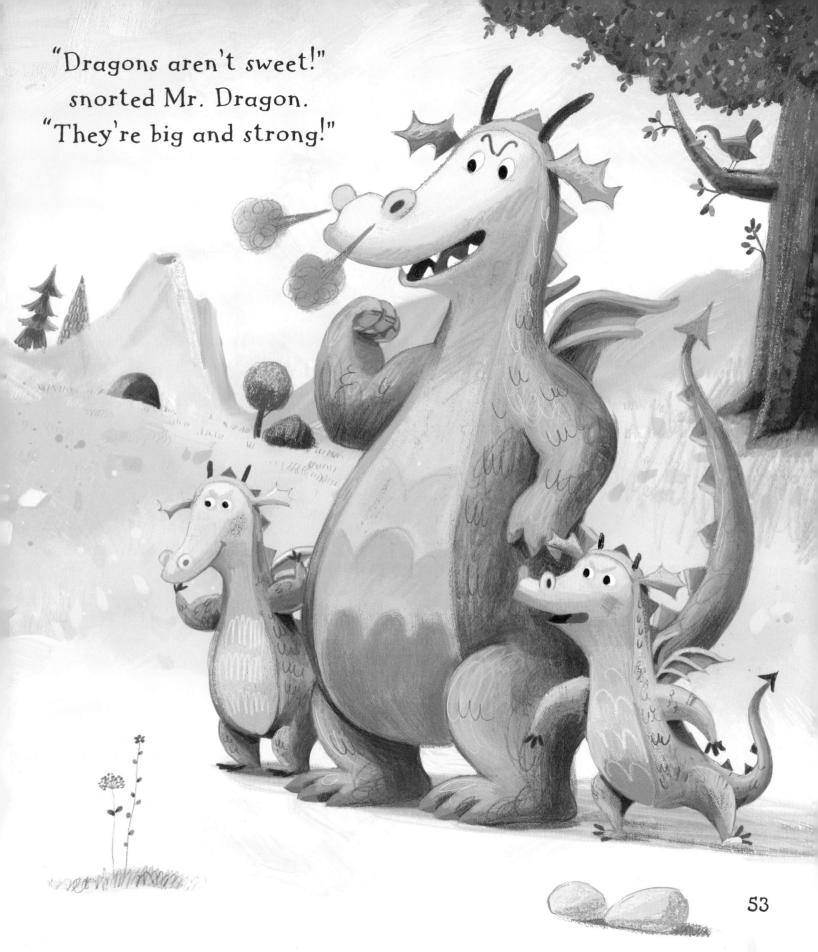

But the Littlest Dragon didn't grow big and strong.

His legs were too
short to run fast.

He was last in
the flying races
because his wings
were too small.

Even worse, he could not breathe fire, however hard he tried.

"Whoever heard of a dragon who can't breathe fire?" laughed the other dragons.

Each day, the Littlest Dragon grew
more sad and lonely. "I'm such a
crummy dragon," he sobbed.

Little Bird fluttered
down from her tree.

56

"I will help you find a way
to **breathe fire**," she said.

"How can you help?" sniffed the Littlest
Dragon. "You're not a dragon!"

"I can be your friend,"
Little Bird replied.

Then winter came.

Mr. and Mrs. Dragon had colds.

The Littlest Dragon's brothers had colds.

And when dragons have colds, they can't breathe fire.
And without their fire, dragons can't keep warm.

"I will find someone to light our fire," said the Littlest Dragon.

And off he went.

The Littlest
Dragon ran
to every house
in the valley.

But every dragon
in the valley had
a cold, and every
fire had gone out.

60

All the dragons were freezing.

"Please help us!" they croaked.

"If only I could breathe fire!" cried the Littlest Dragon.

Suddenly, Little Bird had an idea.

She plucked a feather from her wing and tickled the end of the Littlest Dragon's nose.

The Littlest Dragon's nose began to itch...

The Littlest Dragon's nose began to twitch...

It itched and twitched!

And then...

63

Two fireballs shot out of his nostrils.

"I BREATHED FIRE!"

yelled the Littlest Dragon.

Soon, every dragon in the valley
had a fire to keep them warm.

"You're a hero,"
Mr. Dragon said proudly.

"I could never have done it without Little Bird," the Littlest Dragon replied.

He looked at the feather and smiled.

He might never win running or flying races, but he could breathe fire. And with Little Bird as his friend, he would never be lonely again.

The Greedy Rainbow

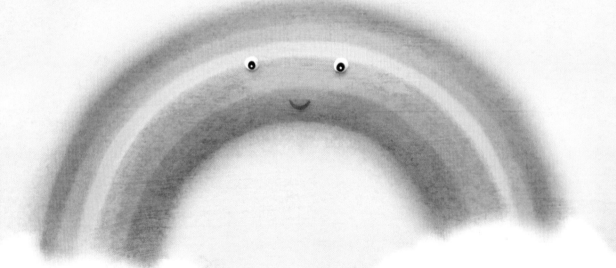

Susan Chandler

Sanja Rešček

Monkey sat at the top of the highest tree in the forest.

Looking around, he spied a tiny rainbow in the leaves.

"What a pretty little
rainbow!" Monkey said.

"I will take you down
to meet my friends."

71

The rainbow bounced
toward him.

"Wrap yourself
around my tail,"
said Monkey.

Then he started climbing
down toward the forest floor.

While they were climbing down,
something strange started happening!

As the rainbow went past,
the red flowers and
green leaves started
losing their colors.

Worse still—
Monkey's golden
fur was fading too!

74

But Monkey didn't notice. He was too busy swinging from branch to branch.

He didn't see the berries' red color fading.

He didn't notice when the orange snake and yellow parrot lost their colors.

As the rainbow went past, the green leaves, blue sky, indigo dragonfly, and violet butterfly all grew dull and lost their colors.

At last, Monkey reached the forest floor.

"Come and meet this little rainbow!" he called to his friends.

But the rainbow wasn't little anymore! It had grown bigger and heavier.

In fact, it was so big that it reached the tops of the trees!

79

The animals gathered around, but the toucan got too close to the rainbow. Her magnificent beak suddenly lost its bright colors.

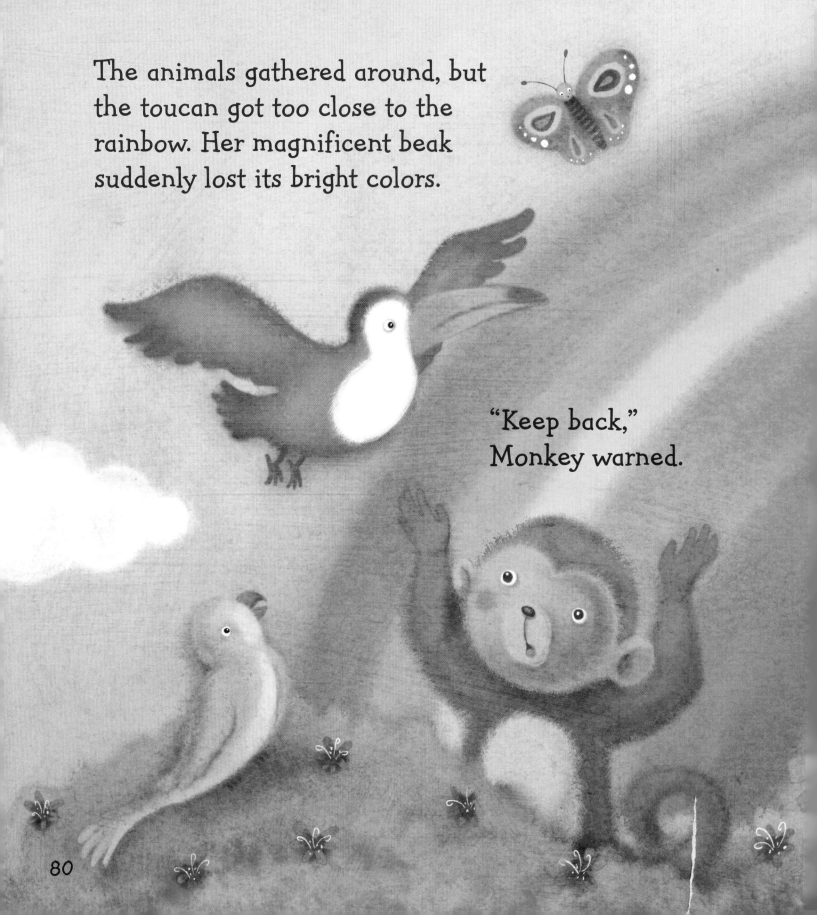

"Keep back," Monkey warned.

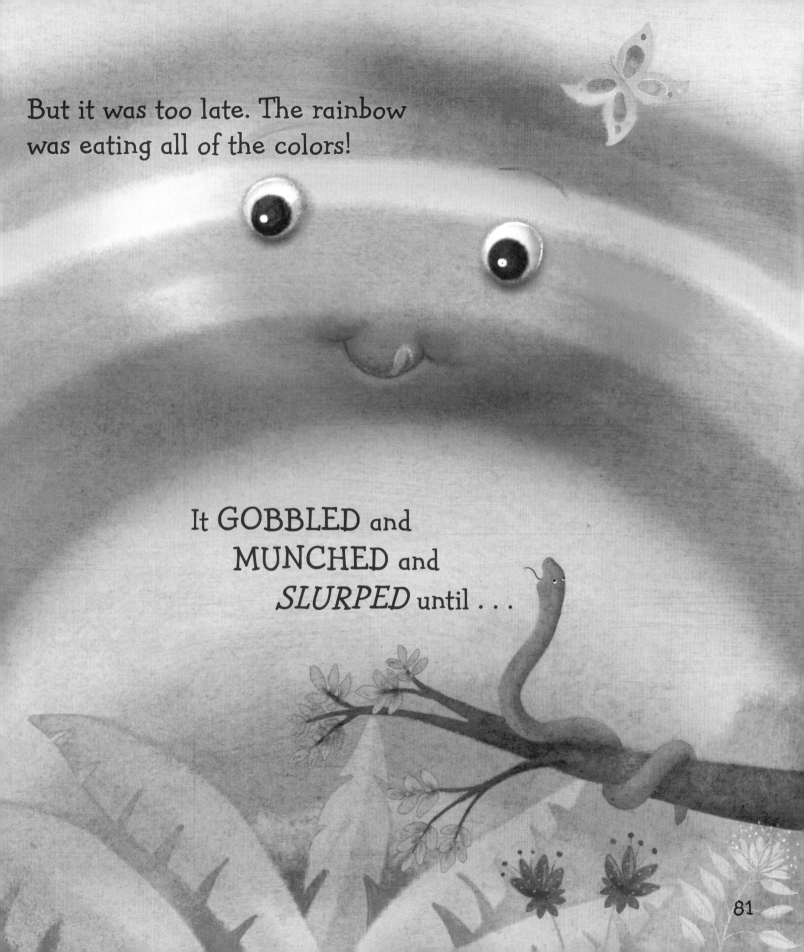

But it was too late. The rainbow was eating all of the colors!

It GOBBLED and MUNCHED and *SLURPED* until . . .

. . . the entire rain forest was gray!

The animals were very sad.

"Look what
you've done!"
cried Monkey.

"You've been so
greedy that you've
eaten all of the colors.
Now there aren't any
left for us to enjoy."

The rainbow gazed down at the rain forest. It wasn't as beautiful without its dazzling colors.

Then the rainbow looked at Monkey and his friends.

It saw how unhappy they were and it felt very bad.

If only it hadn't been so selfish.

The rainbow sighed and sniffed,
then burst into tears!

Big wet drips of red, orange, yellow, green, blue, indigo, and violet splashed onto the forest, soaking everything.

As the rainbow cried, it shrank and drifted high into the forest canopy. It was glad that it had shared the colors with the rain forest.

And of course, everything and everyone got their colors back . . .

. . . just not the same colors they had before!

The lion who lost his ROAR,
but learned to draw

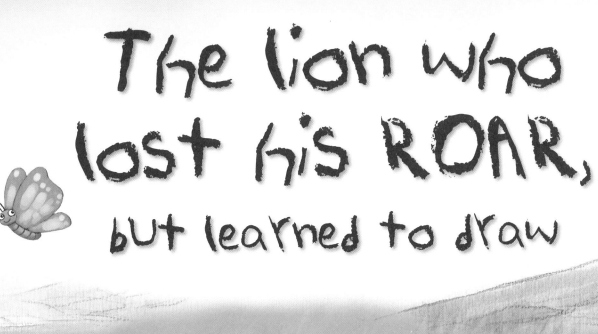

Paula Knight and
Daniel Howarth

"RRRRRROAR!"

Lionel loved to roar.

He had a **deafening** voice.

92

It **startled** butterflies and birds and **scattered** herds of animals.

93

"Please can you **try** to be a little quieter, Lionel?" asked Papa. "You've disturbed the birds, flustered the butterflies, and the zebras are hiding again!"

"RRRRROAR!"

"You're giving me a headache!" said Mama.
"Why don't you sit quietly and draw?"

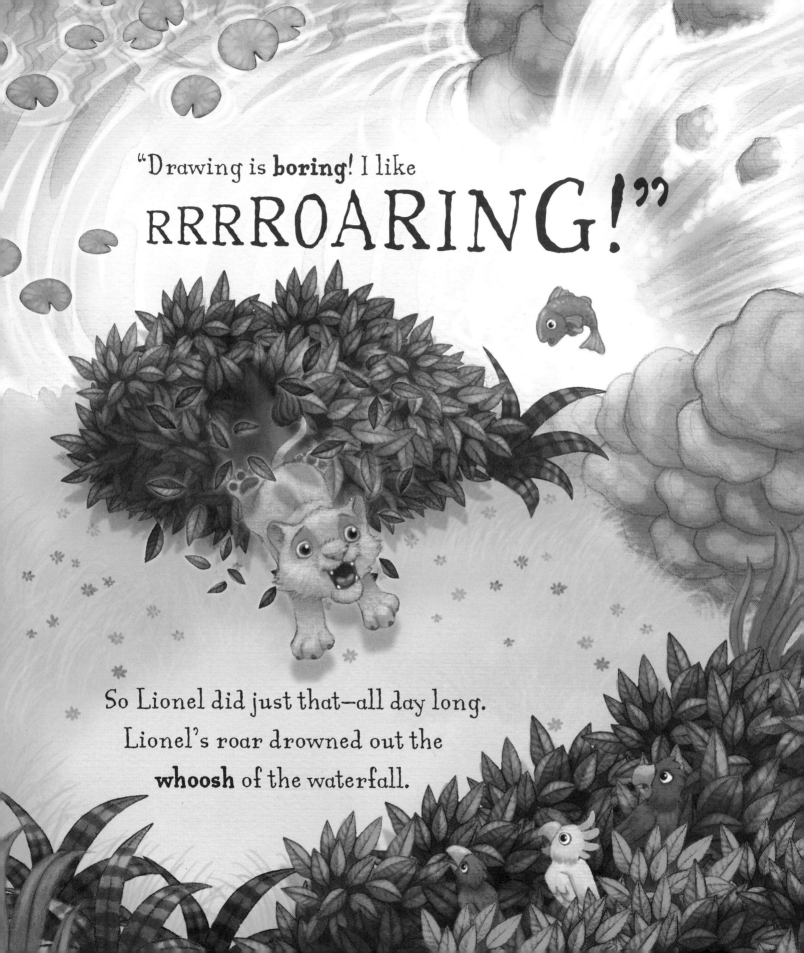

"Drawing is **boring**! I like
RRRROARING!"

So Lionel did just that—all day long.
Lionel's roar drowned out the
whoosh of the waterfall.

He **shocked** a
flock of flamingos.

He **alarmed**
the aardvarks.

He **panicked**
the parrots.

The next morning, Lionel tiptoed
to Mama and Papa's bed.

He opened his mouth . . .

But nothing happened!

His ROAR was no more.

"Oh dear!" Mama said.

"All that roaring has made your throat sore!"

Lionel was thirsty. He pointed to his mouth.
"I don't know what you mean," said Papa.

Lionel went to the lake for a drink.

The flock of flamingos **honked** at him, but Lionel couldn't speak.

The parrots on their
perches said "Squawk,"
but Lionel couldn't reply.

The monkeys **chattered**,
but Lionel was silent.

The elephants **trumpeted**,
but Lionel could only sigh.

101

"Look Lionel,"
said Monkey,
"you've drawn a pattern!"

"It's a curly swirl—just like my tail!"

"Drawn?" thought Lionel.
"But drawing's **boring!**"

"Pretty pattern, pretty pattern!" squawked the parrots.

Lionel had to agree that the pattern did look quite good.

"Can you draw me?" asked Flamingo.

"And me?" added Monkey.

Lionel could only nod.

He bounded home, and the
other animals followed him.

He chose a pink crayon, and started to scribble.

When Lionel handed
over his drawing,
Flamingo was **so** happy.

"Thank you, Lionel.
It looks just like me!"

Drawing was **fun!**

The different-colored crayons matched
the things around him:

Bright blue

Pretty
pink

106

Glossy green

Yummy yellow

107

"How lovely," said Mama.
"You do like drawing, after all!"

"N...n...o,"
Lionel croaked.

His voice was coming back.

Drrrrrroaaaarring!"

The Snake Who Said Shhh

Jodie Parachini

Gill McLean

The jungle was filled with noise on the day Seth was born.

Elephants trumpeted,

Chimpanzees chattered...

Chi-keeee!

E-e-oo-oo

Squawk

Squawk

...and parrots squawked.

Seth slithered out of his leafy hole in the ground.
He stared, wide-eyed, at the trees
and loud animals around him.

Squeak

Mom nudged Seth's slippery body.
"Go on," she said. "Sssay sssomething."

Seth slurped the air with his tongue. Then he let out a big...

"Shhhhhhh!"

"What did he say?"
the parrots squawked.

"You're supposed to say *hiss!*"
growled a grumpy leopard.

118

"Whoever heard of a snake with a lisp?"
cackled the chimpanzees.

Seth blushed.

119

"Don't lisssten to them, ssson," Mom said. "I think you sssound beautiful."

Seth tried again.

"Shhhhhhh," he said.

The baboons fell over
with laughter.

Seth slithered sadly back into his hole.

The jungle burst into a chorus of hoots and howls.

"Enough!" the leopard roared. "We must choose a gift for the new baby."

"How about a toothbrush for his fangs?" suggested a crocodile.

"No," the leopard said.
"An owl feather for his bed.
That's the present we always
give to a new baby snake."

"But I'm old," the owl hooted from his perch.
"I have no spare feathers left to give."

123

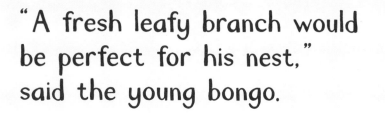

"A fresh leafy branch would be perfect for his nest," said the young bongo.

"Leaves are boring," the chimpanzees complained. "Let's catch him a nice tasty mouse!"

"What?" squeaked the dormouse.
"Let's throw him a party instead.
He can slither and dance and..."

"Snakes can't dance!"
called the sunbird.

125

The animals roared and squawked and chirped and argued, each yelling louder than the next.

They were so busy squabbling that they didn't notice the little snake slide out of his hole.

Grrr!

Snap!

Snap!

As he watched the fuss,
Seth grew sadder
and sadder.

127

At last, he'd had enough.
Seth lifted his head as high
as he could and shouted,

"SHHHHHHHH!"

The jungle
fell silent.

129

"Maybe all he wants is some quiet," whispered the dormouse.

130

The animals looked at each other
and shrugged. No one spoke.
Then they stared at Seth.

Seth licked the air.
Then he snuggled up
with his mom and smiled.

132

"Happy birthday, Seth," the animals whispered. Finally, the jungle was peaceful and still.

SUPERCHIMP

Giles Paley-Phillips

Illustrated by Karl Newson

Way down in the jungle...

...swinging through the trees,

is a **mighty superhero** whose favorite food is fleas.

137

When animals are in trouble
and they give a little **yelp**,

Argh!

138

from out of nowhere, Superchimp
appears to lend his help.

He's **FASTER** than a cheetah

and he's **STRONGER** than a bear.

He can *fly* just like an eagle

and he has red underwear!

Everyone loves Superchimp
because he's strong and brave,

he's got a groovy chimpmobile

and a snazzy secret cave.

When baby Parrot flies too high
and gets stuck in a tree...

...her cries are heard by Superchimp,
who helps to set her free.

When Lion has a splinter,
and Hippo's stuck in muck,

Superchimp's on hand to help,
they just can't believe their luck.

"Superchimp's our hero!"

the animals all rejoice,

but far off in the distance,
they hear a booming voice.

"It's getting rather late young man, I think it's time for bed!"

In the moonlight, Mom appears,
and Superchimp goes red.

Mom gives him a cuddle,
she can see he feels quite shy.

"You can save your friends tomorrow,
for now let's say goodbye."

Being a hero is dangerous,

and it can be really great.

But remember, your mom might get
upset if you ever stay out too late!

154

SNIP SNAP CROC

Caroline Castle
Illustrated by Claire Shorrock

One sunny morning, basking lazily on the sandy banks of the River Nile, lay...

157

...SNIP SNAP CROC!

She swished her huge tail and sang out
to all the creatures on the shore.

"Look at me, I am so fine!
With these big sharp teeth of mine!
Sixty of them go snip, snip, snip!
Come too close and I'll
nip, nip, nip."

In the tall tree, Mama Baboon shivered and told her baby:

"Listen to your mama and stay close by. For I love you more than the mountain is high."

In the bushes, Mama Meerkat told her little ones:

"Don't wander off, keep in my sight.
For **I** love you more than the **stars are bright**."

And in the long grass, Mama Lion
told her bouncy little cubs:

"Don't stray far from your mama's side.
For I love you more than the ocean is wide."

Back on the sandy bank, something strange was happening. Snip Snap Croc heard a little tapping sound.

Underneath her tummy...the ground began to move.

She started to dig, and out of the ground came a clutch of **big, white...**

163

...eggs!

From the eggs
came a sound:

TAP!

TAP!

TAP!

Creatures with little teeth like hammers
were tapping their way out of the eggs.

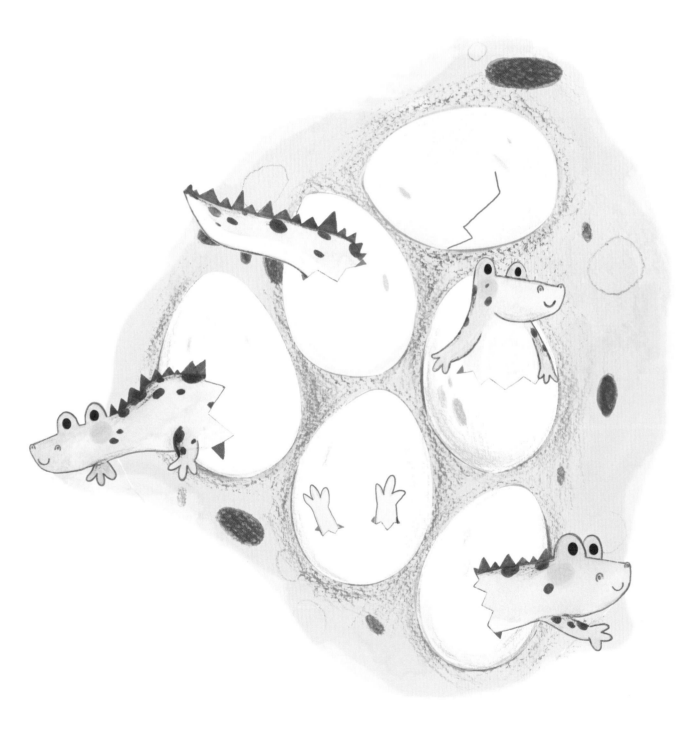

Then, all of a sudden...

...one, two, three, and more little,
baby crocodiles came wriggling
out onto the shore!

Snip Snap Croc was so
happy that she smiled, swished
her huge tail, and cried:

"HOORAY! HOORAY!
Twenty-three babies
born today!"

167

The other little animals watched, as one by one, Snip Snap Croc popped each baby into her mouth!

"Oh, Mama, come quick!" Baby Baboon cried.
"Oh, Mama, over here!" the baby meerkats squealed.
"Oh, Mama," called the lion cubs.

"Do something!"

"Snip Snap Croc is eating her babies!"

But all the other
mamas knew that
Snip Snap Croc had

a secret.

Snip Snap Croc waddled
down to the riverside,
opened her huge mouth,
and carefully popped each
baby into the water!

The newest mama on the riverbank told her babies:

"Stay close by me and
no harm you'll meet.
For I love you more
than the river is deep."

And Mama Baboon,
Mama Meerkat,
and Mama Lion all
sighed happily.

174

They knew Snip Snap Croc loved each of her babies, just as much as any mom.

Mountain high, star bright, ocean wide, and river deep.

An Imprint of Sterling Publishing Co., Inc.
1166 Avenue of the Americas
New York, NY 10036

ISBN: 978-1-4351-6726-1

Manufactured in Guangdong, China
Lot #:
2 4 6 8 10 9 7 5 3 1
10/17

www.sterlingpublishing.com